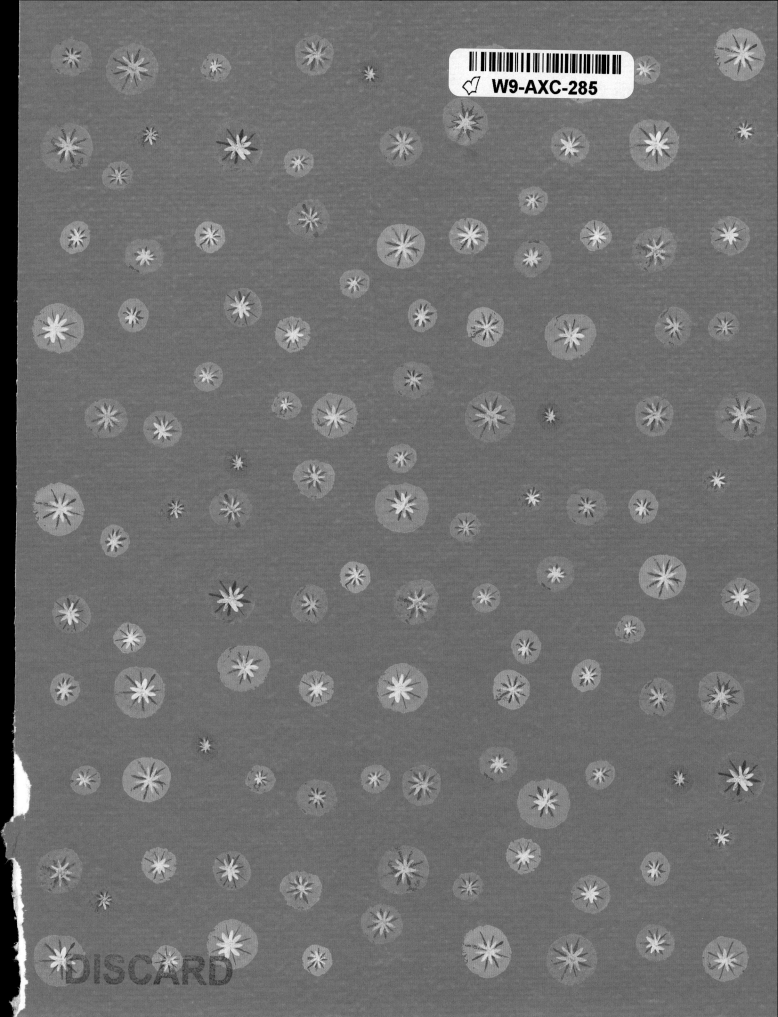

*elsewhere
editions*

MARIO
LEVRERO

DIEGO
BIANKI

SLEEPY STORIES

TRANSLATED FROM THE SPANISH
BY ALICIA LÓPEZ

elsewhere editions

── ONE DAY ──

NICOLÁS: Tell me a story.

ME: No; I'm sleepy.

NICOLÁS: It doesn't matter that you're sleepy. Tell me a story anyway.

ME: Okay, but it's going to be a sleepy story.

NICOLÁS: Yes, yes. It doesn't matter if it's a sleepy story.

ME: Okay. *Yawn*. There was once . . . *yawn* . . . there was once a man who was sleepy. Very sleepy. So sleepy that he couldn't make it all the way home to lie down in his bed and sleep. So . . . *yawn* . . . so he opened the umbrella he was carrying, set it upside down on the ground, and curled up inside it to sleep. And he slept and he slept until it started to rain. And it rained and it rained until the umbrella filled to the brim with water, and the man started to drown and woke himself yelling, "I'm drowning, I'm drowning." Then he clambered up and saw it was raining, and he reached for the umbrella to protect himself from the downpour, but since the umbrella was filled with rain, all the water rushed down and soaked the man even more. And here is where the story ends.

NICOLÁS: Another.

ME: No, no more stories. I'm *very* sleepy.

NICOLÁS: It doesn't matter; it can be a *very* sleepy story then.

ME: But I'm telling you: I'm very, very, very sleepy.

NICOLÁS: But I want a story that is very, very, very sleepy.

ME: Okay. *Yawn*. There . . . *yawn* . . . was . . . *yawn* . . . once *yawn* . . . a maaaan . . . there was once a man who was veeeery sleepy, so veeeeeeeery sleepy . . . *yawn*. He was too sleepy to even move his feet, and since his house was far away, so veeery . . . *yawn* . . . faaaaaar, he started stretching his nose, and he stretched and he stretched his nose, and then he started to stretch his neck, and then his aaaaarms . . . *yawn* . . . and his tooooorso . . . *yawn* . . . and he was streeetching and streeetching, and then he stretched his legs, and first to reach the man's house was his nose and then his head, and the man moved his nose and his head through the window and rested them on the bed; then along came the rest of his body, which had become long and stringy because his feet were still so far away, but his body gradually tucked itself into bed; and at last, when everything except his feet was resting in bed, his feet unstuck themselves from the ground and his legs sprung back toward his body like a rubber band and joined the rest of him in bed, and the man fell asleep, and here is where the story ends.

NICOLÁS: Another.

—— ANOTHER DAY ——

NICOLÁS: Tell me a sleepy story.

ME: No, because I'm very sleepy, and if I tell you a sleepy story I'll get even sleepier.

NICOLÁS: It doesn't matter; I want you to tell me a sleepy story and get even sleepier, so then you can tell me a story that's even sleeeeeepier.

ME: Okay. There was once . . . *yawn* . . . a man . . . *yawn* . . . a man who was sleepy; he was very sleepy, so sleepy . . . *yawn* . . . so, so sleepy, that he couldn't even see; and he thought he'd made it home and was opening his own door and lying down in his own bed, but really . . . *yawn* . . . really he was at the zoo and had opened the monkey cage and lain down in the monkeys' bed and as soon as the monkeys saw him . . . *yawn* . . . they picked him up and decided to have some fun. They grabbed him by the legs and tossed him up, another monkey caught him in mid-air with her tail and swung him upside down for a while then let him fall, and another monkey caught him and shook him and rolled him across the floor like a ball, pushing him around the cage with his feet.

NICOLÁS: Monkeys don't have feet.

ME: Well, they were pushing him with the hands on their hind legs then — until the man realized he was being rolled and tossed around for the monkeys' amusement and he ran out of the cage, and now he was even sleepier than before and couldn't see at all, and he entered the seal tank, and right away the seals decided to have some fun with him too, and they started spinning him around on the tips of their noses, but the man was so sleepy, so, so, so sleepy, that he fell asleep even as he spun on the seals' noses, and he slept and he slept and he slept until at last he woke up and made his way home, and this is where the story ends.

NICOLÁS: Another.

ME: No.

NICOLÁS: But I want *another* story.

ME: No, because I'm *really* sleepy; very, very, very sleepy.

NICOLÁS: I don't care that you're sleepy.

ME: But the story would be a story that is also *really* very, very, very sleepy.

NICOLÁS: And I want a story that is *really* very, very, very sleepy.

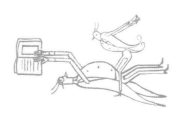

ME: Well. Turns out that . . . *yawn* . . . there was . . . *yawn* . . . once . . . *yawn* . . . a . . . man . . . who . . . *yawn* . . . *snores.*

NICOLÁS: Hey! Don't fall asleep! Keep going with the story!

ME: There was once . . . *yawn* a man who was so sleepy . . . *yawn* . . . so very very very sleepy . . . that he couldn't bear so much sleepiness and wanted to get to his house quickly and so . . . *yawn* . . . *deep sigh* . . .

NICOLÁS: Hey!

ME: *jolt* . . . so he got on a skateboard that a boy had left on the street and since the whole street was downhill he rolled all the way to his house, but he was so sleepy, so very very very sleepy, that he fell asleep right there on the skateboard and rolled and rolled downhill until he reached the sea and tumbled into the water and fell asleep at the bottom of the ocean. Suddenly a little fish came along and tapped him on the shoulder: "Sir, sir, if you fall asleep at the bottom of the ocean you are going to drown," and the man woke up yelling: "Help, I'm drowning," and he sputtered to the surface, swam and swam and swam, and when he got to the beach he fell asleep, and this is where the story ends . . . *snores*

NICOLÁS: Another.

— ANOTHER DAY —

NICOLÁS: I want a sleepy story, and then another veeeeeery veeeeeery sleepy one, and then another that is really very, very, very sleepy.

ME: Well. There was once a man . . . *yawn* . . . a man . . . *yawn* . . . a man who was very, so very sleepy. So he went home and lay down and fell asleep . . . *yawn* . . . *grunt* . . . *deep sigh* . . . *snore.*

NICOLÁS: Hey! Hey, hey, hey! HEY!

ME: *jolt* . . . then, when the man was really, truly fast asleep, a robber came in through the window and started to take everything. He took the little spoons and handed them to another robber, who was standing outside waiting — and this other robber took them and placed them one after another in a big truck — and then the cups, and the big spoons, and the forks, and the knives, and then the dresser, and then the table along with everything that was on it, and the curtains, and the rug, and the sofa, and the chairs, and he passed everything through the window, even the nails where the picture frames had hung, and then he slipped the blankets from beneath the man who was still asleep and was . . . *yawn* . . . still very sleepy . . . *yawn* . . . very, so very, so very sleepy . . . *yawn* . . . *silence.*

Nicolás: And?

Me: *silence*

Nicolás: Hey, hey, hey, HEY! The story! Hey!

Me: . . . and the man went on sleeping, and sleeping, and the robber slid the bedsheets, and the pillow, and the mattress, and then the bed out from under him, and then he passed the sleeping man through the window, and they put him in the truck with all of his things and took it all away. But a few police officers came along and stopped them — "what do you have there" — and made them open the doors of the truck and when the policemen saw they had stolen everything, they waved their batons at the robbers menacingly and told them to put everything back as it was before. So then the robbers went back and returned each thing to its place, and then they put the man back in bed and covered him with his bedsheet and blanket, and then the policemen arrested the robbers and took them away. And when the man woke up, he said, "I slept so well," and here is where the story ends.

Nicolás: Another.

ME: No, look, I'm veeeeeery, so veeeeeeeeeery, veeeeeeeeeeeeeeeeeeery sleepy . . .

NICOLÁS: I don't care. I want a story that is veeeeeery, so veeeeeeeeeeery, veeeeeeeeeeeeeeeeeeeeeeery sleepy.

ME: Okay *yawn*. There . . . *yawn* . . . was . . . *yawn* . . . once . . . *yawn* . . . a man who was veeeeeeeery . . . *yawn* so veeeeeeery sleepy. So sleepy that he told himself: "I'm going to take a bus home, and then go to bed." And the bus came and the man got on and sat at the back and fell asleep, and he slid down his seat so he was hidden from sight, slumping in the back of the bus. So the bus reached its final destination and turned back around and then the bus driver saw the slumped, sleeping man and woke him up and made him get off. The man told himself: "But, I'm even further away from my house than before," and he took another bus, and the same thing happened again, and he took another, and the same thing happened once more, and the man kept getting off at the same spot; until at last, having slept so much on all those bus rides, he felt well-rested and walked home, and this is where the story ends.

NICOLÁS: Another.

MARIO LEVRERO wrote short stories, novels, science fiction, comic books, and crossword puzzles. He was interested in self-hypnosis, believed in telepathy, loved science, hated being addressed in the "usted" form, could not abide solemnity in general. He read detective novels, even at breakfast. He loved movies and tango music. He admired Mandrake the Magician, Lewis Carroll, and the Beatles. Alvaro Enrigue said, "We are all Mario Levrero's children."

As a child I liked to draw, and would sketch all day: in my school notebooks, on the walls of my room, phone books, or on discarded paper from my father's printing press.

At home (and at the printing press, which was like a second home), I would spend hours and hours playing with pencils, crayons, paintbrushes, and even small slivers of red bricks I would use to draw on the street. My parents always encouraged this interest, which grew and grew over time until it became my job.

When I finished my studies, I left my small hometown for the big city of Buenos Aires, where I drew for newspapers, magazines, CD's, theater sets, and books. This book is special to me because through it I found a new way to have fun — playing with the tonalities of sunsets and the deep blue of cloudless nights in the city where I live. The sun and the moon were two important friends to me as I looked for the exact colors to illustrate these "sleepy" stories.

—DIEGO BIANKI

When I was little, I was certain that being in the ocean for long enough would change me into something slick and dexterously fishy. I would tumble out of the car, slip into the water, and feel the ocean around me shimmering with this possibility. My parents would wade in with food held over their heads because I wouldn't come out, not even to eat. I was waiting for my hands to go soft and wrinkled – surely signaling I would transform if I stayed just a little longer underwater. I remember sneaking out for a moonlit swim when I was ten, certain I would stay submerged long enough at last. And I remember the moment I gave up on my project – the realization that my fingers went just as wrinkly in the ocean as they did in the green bathtub of our new home or in the sharply chlorinated pool where I took swim lessons on Tuesdays.

—ALICIA LÓPEZ

Elsewhere Editions
232 Third Street #A111
Brooklyn, NY 11215
www.elsewhereeditions.org

Funding for the translation of this book was provided by a grant from the Carl
Lesnor Family Foundation. This work was made possible by the New York
State Council on the Arts with the support of Governor Andrew M. Cuomo
and the New York State Legislature.

Archipelago Books also gratefully acknowledges the generous support of
Lannan Foundation, Anne and Nick Germanacos, the National Endowment
for the Arts, and the New York City Department of Cultural Affairs.

PRINTED IN CHINA

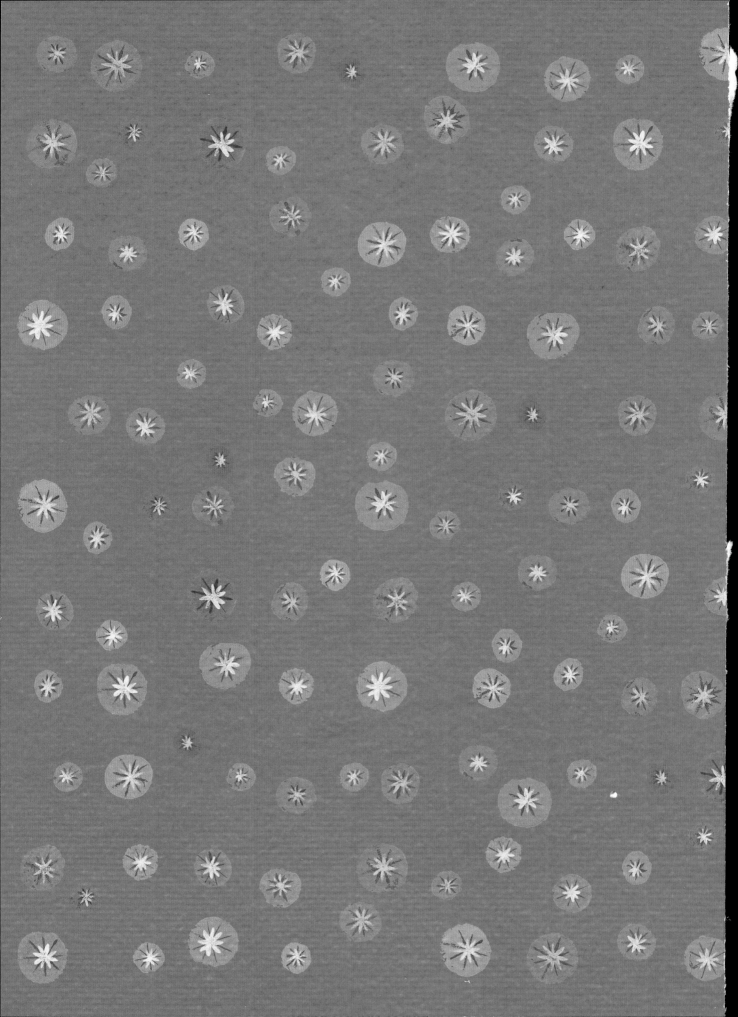